Mocha
The *Real Doctor*

Dedication

This book is for Katie Bacon Robinson,
who loved all creatures great and small. J.R.W.

For Idamay and Charlie with love
and thanks for everything. M.H.

Acknowledgment

Jane Roberts Wood frequently visits the animal clinic of her daughter, Dr. Susan Read, who is not only a *real* doctor but a *good* doctor. Dr. Read advised her mother that the turtle had pneumonia, the fish a dizzy bladder, and the rabbit an abscess. The kittens were left on the doorstep.

bright sky press
Box 416
Albany, Texas 76430

Text copyright © 2003 by Jane Roberts Wood
Illustrations copyright © 2003 by Mary Haverfield

10 9 8 7 6 5 4 3 2 1

Library of Congress Cataloging-in-Publication Data

Wood, Jane Roberts, 1929–
    Mocha , the real doctor / by Jane Roberts Wood ; illustrated by Mary Haverfield.
      p. cm.
    Summary: Mocha, an injured cat who finds a home at an animal clinic, makes nighttime doctor rounds there and helps the various animals.
    ISBN 1-931721-30-0
    [1. Cats—Fiction. 2. Animal rescue—Fiction. 3. Veterinarians—Fiction.] I. Title: Mocha. II. Haverfield, Mary, ill. III. Title.

PZ7.W84962Mo 2003
[E]—dc21

                           2003049565

Book and cover design by Isabel Lasater Hernandez

Printed in China through Asia Pacific Offset

Mocha
The *Real Doctor*

by
Jane Roberts Wood

Illustrated by
Mary Haverfield

Mocha, a soft yellow cat, sleeps in a yellow basket at Dr. Susan's animal clinic. While Mocha sleeps, boys and girls come, bringing their pets in to see the doctor. They bring their cats and their dogs. Their rabbits and their fish. Their hamsters and their birds. And all day long Mocha sleeps and sleeps.

At the end of one very long day, the sun went down. And the girl who walked the dogs went home. And the technician who gave the shots went home. And the boy who cleaned the cages went home. And Dr. Susan got in her car and drove away.

And then …

Mocha sprang to his feet and straightened his tail!

And Mocha the *Real Doctor* went on his rounds!

First, he stopped by the very small cage of a very small turtle. The turtle had a cold. It would not eat. It would not come out of its shell. Mocha snuggled up close and began to purr. The little turtle hidden away inside his shell heard Mocha's song. Mocha sang about a cool, still pool of water.

The little turtle stuck one foot out.

Mocha purred about bugs in a muddle and frogs in a puddle.

The little turtle put another foot out.

Mocha sang about ferns growing wild in an oozy bog
and ladybugs flying 'round an old oak log.
The little turtle stuck its head out. And then ...
The very small turtle began to eat!

Next Mocha stopped by a small rabbit's cage. The little white rabbit had a sore foot. It could not hop. Mocha purred about buttercups and bluebonnets and flutter mills and daisy wheels.

The bunny licked his sore foot.

Mocha purred about the rich smells of mesquite trees and sassafras leaves.

The bunny sniffed the air. He put his sore foot down.

Then Mocha purred a crisp song about green lettuce and black-eyed peas and sweet corn grown as high as your knees. And then ...

The little bunny hopped a very small hop!

Then Doctor Mocha stopped by the cage of three tiny kittens. The kittens were so young their eyes had not opened. They did not know how to drink milk from a saucer. Mocha opened the door of the cage and went inside. He drew the kittens close and bathed their closed-up-tight eyes. Then he sang about pouncing on strings and birds that sing.

The kittens snuggled underneath his throat.

Mocha purred about chasing tails and playing with snails.

One by one the kittens opened their round, blue eyes.